For Simon, Alison, and Laura
—A. H. B.

For Maxim and Olivia
—E. H.

Text copyright © 1998 by A. H. Benjamin
Illustrations copyright © 1998 by Elisabeth Holstien

This 2004 edition published by Backpack Books,
by arrangement with Magi Publications, London.

Backpack Books
122 Fifth Avenue, New York, NY 10011

ISBN 0-7607-5977-4

Printed and bound in Singapore

04 05 06 07 08 [Imago] 10 9 8 7 6 5 4 3 2 1

First published in Great Britain 1998 by Little Tiger Press,
an imprint of Magi Publications, London

A. H. Benjamin and Elisabeth Holstien have asserted
their rights to be identified as the author and illustrator
of this work under the Copyright, Designs and
Patents Act, 1988.

A DUCK SO SMALL

by A.H. Benjamin
Pictures by Elisabeth Holstien

BACKPACKBOOKS
•
NEW YORK

Duffle was a very small duck,
and all the other ducks laughed
at him because of his size.

"A duck so small can do nothing
at all!" they jeered.
   I may be small, thought Duffle sadly,
but there must be *something* I can do.
He wondered what it could be.

Duffle looked around and noticed
Kingfisher perched on a reed. He was
just about to say hello when . . .

Kingfisher suddenly took off and dived,
straight as an arrow, into the water.
Kingfisher is small, thought Duffle, but he
dives well. Perhaps I could do that, too.

"Look what I can do!" Duffle
called out to the other ducks.
He flew high into the air . . .

and came down again
like a falling rock.

Duffle hit the water and did a reverse
belly flop.

"Ha-ha, what did we say," cried the other
ducks. "A duck so small can do nothing at all!"

Poor Duffle felt very foolish.
He climbed out onto the
riverbank and wondered
what to do next.

Duffle saw Heron standing perfectly still on one leg in the shallow water. What good balance she has, thought Duffle. Perhaps I could do that, too.

"Look what I can do!"
Duffle called as he stood
on one leg with his wings
spread out.

He wobbled this
way and that and . . .

landed flat on his beak.

"Ha-ha, what did we say," laughed the other ducks. "A duck so small can do nothing at all!"

Duffle crept into the shade of a nearby tree so
the others wouldn't see him blush. He heard a *tap,
tap, tap* above his head.

Looking up, Duffle saw Woodpecker making a hole
in the trunk. What a strong beak he has, thought the
little duck. Perhaps I could bore a hole, too.

"Look what I can do!" Duffle called out to the other ducks. He flew up into the tree and perched on a thick branch. *Peck, peck, peck*, he chipped at the wood.

"Oops," he cried as he lost his balance. Duffle toppled from the branch and . . .

fell to the ground.

"Ha-ha, what did we say," cackled the other ducks.
"A duck so small can do nothing at all!"

All the other ducks were paddling and splashing in the river, but poor Duffle decided to hide in the rushes until they left. That way he wouldn't have to listen to their teasing.

I'm not good at anything.
I'm just a small useless duck,
he thought. And a tear rolled
down his beak.

For a long time Duffle heard the other ducks quacking with laughter. It seemed as though they would never leave.

Then he listened again, and they weren't laughing anymore.

They were quacking in alarm!

Duffle paddled over to see what all the fuss
was about. The other ducks were crowded around
a tiny hole in the riverbank where a duckling had
gotten stuck.

"Oh, please get him out," begged the duckling's
mother.

"We will," said the other ducks, but it was no use.
They were just too big to squeeze into the hole.

All except for Duffle.
"Let *me* try," he said, and because
he was so small, he was able to
reach right in.

It didn't take him long
to rescue the trapped
duckling.

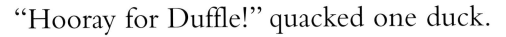

"Hooray for Duffle!" quacked one duck.
"None of us could have done that," said another.
"A duck so small *can* do something after all!"
cried a third.

"Oh, it was nothing," blushed Duffle. But he knew it *was* something, and after that the other ducks never made fun of him again.